Contents

Meet Emily. Her grandfather owns Adventure Park. It's the best theme park in the world!

Meet Jacob. He's Emily's best friend.

Meet Frank. He's Emily's pet hamster.

Together, they test Adventure Park's new rides.

Some of the rides are magical. Some of the rides are scary. Some of the rides are dangerous. But ALL of the rides are exciting!

Join Emily, Jacob and Frank on the adventure of a lifetime.

ADVENTURE PARK

CANDY CRISIS

By Cavan Scott • Illustrated by Abby Ryder

Titles in the Adventure Park set

Dinosaur Danger

Monster Mayhem

Pirate Peril

Candy Crisis

Chaos

t Riot

Medieval Madness

Pyramid Panic

Badger Publishing Limited,
Oldmedow Road, Hardwick Industrial Estate,
King's Lynn PE30 4JJ

Telephone: 01438 791037
www.badgerlearning.co.uk

2 4 6 8 10 9 7 5 3 1

Candy Crisis ISBN 978-1-78464-339-3

Text © Cavan Scott 2016
Complete work © Badger Publishing Limited 2016

Publisher: Susan Ross
Senior Editor: Danny Pearson
Editorial Coordinator: Claire Morgan
Illustration: Abby Ryder
Designer: Bigtop Design

Cast of Characters

Emily

Jacob

Frank

Vocabulary

chuckled – laughed quietly.

summit – the top of a mountain.

galloped – ran like a horse.

revenge – to harm someone because they've harmed you.

liquorice – a chewy sweet.

lava – hot, molten rock.

fray – to unravel or come apart.

CHAPTER 1 Popping Candy

"It's hot!" Frank the hamster squealed. "Too hot!"

"Of course it's hot," Emily snapped. "We're hanging over a volcano. What do you expect?"

She was dangling from a rope with her best friend Jacob.

Beneath them, steam rose up from a lake of hot lava. Their arms were tied and there was no way to climb back up the rope to safety.

They were trapped and running out of ideas.

"We need to do something fast!" Jacob said, looking up.

The rope that was holding them was starting to come apart. If it snapped, they'd plunge into the boiling liquid far below.

But wait! We've skipped to the end of the story.

Why are Emily, Jacob and Frank hanging over a bubbling volcano? And who has tied them up?

Well, it all began when Frank was trying some of Adventure Park's new popcorn.

"This is delicious," he said, offering some to Emily.

She took a handful. Frank was right. It was wonderful. Really sweet!

Suddenly, there was a noise from above. Emily looked up to see Albert Sparkle-Trousers flying through the air. He was wearing a rocket jetpack.

Albert was Emily's grandfather and the owner of Adventure Park.

He was also out of control.

"He's going to crash!" shouted Jacob.

Sure enough, smoke was pouring out of the back of the jetpack.

Albert was spinning around and around. With a cry, the old man dropped into a dive. He was heading straight for them!

"Quick! Out of the way!" Jacob said, pushing Emily aside.

BANG!

Albert smacked into the ground, right where Emily had been standing.

When the dust settled, Albert was laughing. "That was brilliant!" he chuckled. "I must do it again!"

Frank wasn't so happy. "You made me spill my popcorn!" the hamster squeaked.

The sweet snack was all over the floor.

"Not to worry," said Albert. He took off his tall hat to reveal a big box of corn. "Here, take this. You can pop it when you get home!"

Frank took the box happily. Carefully, he stored it in his cheeks for later. Frank could keep all kinds of things in his cheeks. They were a little bit magic.

"You're in a good mood, Mr S!" said Jacob.

Albert grinned. "It's because of my new ride, the Rainbow Roller! Would you like to give it a try?"

CHAPTER 2 The Rainbow Roller

Soon, Emily, Jacob and Frank were being strapped into a rollercoaster.

There was something very different about this ride. Instead of rails, the rollercoaster ran on a rainbow!

"Are you ready?" Albert asked.

"Yes!" the children replied, excitedly.

Albert pulled a lever and they were off. The rollercoaster sped forward. It climbed up the rainbow going faster and faster.

"This is amazing!" Emily shouted.

"I can't wait to go down the other side!" Jacob replied.

The rollercoaster reached the top of the rainbow and started racing back down again.

"Weeeeeeeeee!" the children cheered.

But Frank didn't say a word. He had noticed something ahead.

"There's a crack in the rainbow!" he squeaked in alarm.

The children gasped as they saw that he was right.

There was no time to react. The rollercoaster hit the crack and the rainbow shattered.

They tumbled from the sky, falling down and down and down.

CHAPTER 3 Candy Land!

BOING!

The rollercoaster car hit the ground, but didn't break up.

The ground wasn't hard. It was spongy. They bounced back up into the air and came down gently.

"Where are we?" Jacob asked.

Emily leaned out of the rollercoaster and prodded the ground. "It's made of jelly!" she said.

"Jelly?" Frank asked and dived off the side of the rollercoaster.

He plopped into the jelly and started to eat!
"It's apple flavour!" he said with his mouth full.

Jacob ate a handful himself. "No it's not. It's orange!" he argued.

Emily tried some too. This time, it tasted like strawberry!

"But that's impossible," she said.

Jacob looked around. "It's *all* impossible. Look at this place!"

Everywhere they turned there were sweets.

Lollipops grew from marshmallow hills like flowers. Trees and bushes had jellybeans instead of leaves. Even the clouds looked like candyfloss.

It was like a dream come true. Brightly coloured butterflies flew through the air and unicorns galloped in the fields.

The three friends scrambled up a hill and started eating. Everything tasted as good as it looked.

"This is your grandfather's best ride yet," said Frank happily. "Even if the rollercoaster did crash!"

Jacob spotted something on the horizon. A group of people were rushing towards them. No, they weren't people. They were bears. Gummy bears!

"Just when you thought this place couldn't get any weirder!" Emily laughed.

She waved at the gummy bears. 'Hello!"

The bears didn't wave back. They hurried up to the children, led by a larger bear.

This one wore a big wobbly crown and carried a long stick of rock.

Jacob took a step towards them. "My name's Jacob," he said, "and these are my friends, Emily and Frank."

The large gummy bear smiled sweetly. "I'm the Candy Queen and this is my Candy Kingdom."

"And a wonderful kingdom it is, too!" said Frank, his mouth stuffed with jellybeans.

"Oh, do you think so?" asked the queen.

"Yes," nodded Emily.

"That's good to hear," the queen said, before her smile faded. "Because you're never going to leave. Guards, take them!"

All at once, the other gummy bears rushed forwards and grabbed the three friends.

"What are you doing?" asked Jacob. He struggled against the bears, but couldn't break free. "Let us go!"

The queen grinned again. This time the smile wasn't sweet at all. "Never!" she snapped. "You're all under arrest!"

 **CHAPTER 4** Sweet Revenge

"I don't understand," said Emily as they were dragged up the side of a tall mountain. "We haven't done anything wrong!"

"Haven't done anything wrong?" the queen repeated. "Of course, you have. You're children!"

"And what's wrong with being a child?" Jacob asked.

The queen stopped and faced them. "What's wrong?" she screeched. "Tell me, what do children do?"

Emily shrugged. "Play?" she suggested.

"No!" the queen snapped back.

"Make noise?" Jacob said.

"No!" the queen shouted.

Frank sighed. He'd worked it out. "They eat sweet things," he said sadly.

"Exactly!" yelled the queen. "Gummy bears. chocolate bunnies. Jelly babies. And now I'm going to take revenge!"

The friends were dragged up to the top of the mountain. Smoke was blowing from its summit.

Emily's eyes widened when she realised what she was looking at. "Wait a minute!" she said. "This isn't just a mountain. It's a volcano!"

"A *sugar* volcano!" the queen laughed. "And you're going to be thrown into it!"

The gummy bears tied the friends together with liquorice rope and dragged them to the mouth of the volcano.

Deep below, hot sugary lava bubbled in the heart of the mountain.

"You can't do this to us," Emily shouted.

"Watch me!" the queen said, and shoved them over the edge!

CHAPTER 5 Into the Volcano

The three friends tumbled into the volcano.

They screamed all the way.

"AAAAAAAAARGH!"

Suddenly, they jolted to a halt. Emily looked up. They were dangling from a long rope. High above them, the Candy Queen laughed.

"This serves you right!" she shouted. "All those years of eating sweets. Now when this rope snaps, you'll be candy-coated yourselves!"

Emily looked at the rope. It was already starting to fray.

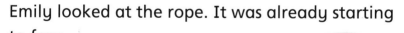

"If that thing breaks, we'll fall into the boiling sugar!" Jacob said.

But Emily had a plan.

"Frank," she said. "Do you still have the box of corn that Grandad gave you?"

Frank wriggled his paws free and checked. "Yes," he said, pulling the box out of his cheeks. "How will that help?"

"Pour it into the volcano!" Emily told him.

Frank's face fell. "Really? I was saving it for later."

"There won't *be* a later if we get cooked!" Jacob reminded him.

Grumbling, Frank threw the corn box into the volcano.

The sugar lava rumbled.

The sugar lava bubbled.

The sugar lava belched.

"Hold on!" Emily shouted. "This could get bumpy!"

"Why?" asked Frank. "What's going to happen?"

Deep below them, something started to pop.

And pop.

And POP.

And POP!

WHOOSH!

Without warning, a cloud of popcorn shot up towards them.

It pushed them out of the volcano and high into the sky.

On the side of the mountain, the Candy Queen hopped around in fury. "Come back!" she shouted after them. "I want to have my revenge!"

Then some popcorn plopped into her open mouth. She licked her lips. "That is delicious!" she said, completely forgetting about the children. "Everyone, dive in!"

Obeying their queen, the gummy bears of the Candy Kingdom jumped into the volcano and started eating.

Meanwhile, Emily, Jacob and Frank were thrown all the way back to Adventure Park. The ground rushed towards them as they tumbled down from the sky.

"I hate heights," Frank wailed, "especially when I'm falling from them!"

"What are we going to do?" yelled Jacob.

"Let me help!" said a voice. Albert Sparkle-Trousers rocketed up to them using his jetpack. He caught the three friends and brought them safely back to the ground.

"What an adventure," Emily sighed.

"Here," said Albert, offering them three bags of popcorn. "This should make you feel better."

Frank wrinkled his nose. "Thanks, but no thanks," he said, pushing the popcorn away. "I think I've lost my sweet tooth, for a while at least!"

Questions

1. What was under Albert Sparkle-Trousers' hat? (*page 10*)

2. What did the rollercoaster run on? (*page 12*)

3. What was growing on the trees in the Candy Kingdom? (*page 16*)

4. Why did the Candy Queen want revenge? (*page 21*)

5. How did the friends escape the volcano? (*page 28*)

6. Who caught the children as they fell from the sky? (*page 29*)

Meet the Author

Cavan Scott spends his days making up stuff – and he loves it! He's written for *Star Wars*, *Doctor Who*, *Adventure Time*, *Skylanders*, *Angry Birds*, *Penguins of Madagascar* and *The Beano*! He lives in Bristol with his wife, daughters and an inflatable Dalek called Desmond!

Meet the Illustrator

Abby Ryder is a cartoonist who loves comic books and video games. Her greatest life ambition is to one day become best friends with a giant robot.